2020, An Obese Turtle

101 COVID Words and Phrases We Want to Forget

The Wordsworth Collective

This book is dedicated to all the frontline and essential workers to whom we owe such a debt of gratitude. Thank you.

Preface

Let's face it, we've all had enough. 2020 is a year we all want to forget. Plans canceled, beards grown, jobs lost, restaurants closed, zoom meetings in your underwear, no toilet roll in the supermarket, the list is endless. New words and phrases we had never heard of suddenly became mainstream, from social distancing to flattening the curve, to covidiots and zumping. But let's not forget the hundreds of thousands of lives ruined and lost.

This book in no way seeks to diminish the horrific impact of COVID-19 around the world on so many families. It is designed to provide a little levity in a time of grief, to help those who need a respite from the doom and gloom that was 2020. It was a horrible year. If years had awards this year would win the Worst Year of the 21st Century Award. The 'You Suck' Year Award. This year would be single if years could date. This year would wear a cone of shame. You get the idea. Sorry 2020, but you won't be missed. 2021, you have a very low bar to live up to.

This book contains a little adult language, but not much. A percentage of all profits will be donated to doctors and nurses to whom we all owe a debt of gratitude.

The Wordsworth Collective

Quarantine

This word used to be for sad-faced puppies coming into the country, or sci-fi alien spaceship dramas. We never want to hear it again. Even if it's in a Taylor Swift romantic ballad.

The 'R' Number

We've lived our entire lives not knowing about R numbers or caring. Let's give the R number a new definition. Maybe the number of 'Arr's' pirates say in a sentence?

Flattening the Curve

A year ago it sounded like an innocent jibe for someone with a big bouncy belly. Now we just want to live a curve free life. No more flattening, unless you're making pancakes.

Social Distancing

It used to be called being lonely. Now it's science and the law.

6ft Rule

Originally invented by strip clubs to keep the pervs at a safe distance. Also minimum height requirements for basketball players and signs on very low bridges. Now it's how we make babies.

Lockdown

This is the 2020 word of the year. Lockdown was for naughty prisoners. Now the whole world is a naughty prisoner.

Zoom

We all went from happy-go-lucky Zoom free lives to Zoom everything. Zoom yoga, weddings, funerals, parties, dates, to every TV news anchor on bad Zoom connections. We've done enough Zooming for one lifetime thank you.

Masks

Masks were for Eyes Wide Shut parties, surgeons and the Phantom of the Opera. Let's give the term back to them.

Vaccine

2021 is going to be Christmas every day for the anti-vaxers. No matter how many lives are saved, someone, somewhere, will have anti-Covid vaccine issues that they feel they need to make a banner for and shout very loudly at passers by.

Antibodies

We're not quite sure what they are, or if we have them, but they may be a good thing, perhaps. Antipasta was hard enough to get our heads around. Is it pasta or not?

Maskhole

An 'idiot' (and we are being VERY kind here) who chose not to wear a mask for a variety of reasons. But pretty much comes down to stupidity.

Shitshow

2020 has had too many shitshows. The shitshow became mainstream. It even became a wine. Shitshow sums up the year quite well.

Quarantine and Chill

Netflix and Chill was so simple and innocent. Quarantine and chill? Isn't that like telling a claustrophobic person in a very small room to just relax? No thank you.

CDC

The CDC only had one job - controlling disease. If you don't do your job, perhaps there's something fundamentally very wrong? If you build a rocket to the moon and it never gets off the launch pad, perhaps you shouldn't be in the space business? If you're a shepherd and all your sheep hate you, perhaps you shouldn't tend to sheep? If you think you're a comedian and no one ever laughs at your jokes, maybe you shouldn't be President?

Covidiot

Who knew 2020 would see a word for selfish people who hoard toilet rolls in their basement? This lovely term was also used for those who insisted on shaking hands even though that could kill someone. We think 'murderer' sounds better than Covidiot.

Moronavirus

Those stupid idiots who tested positive and still denied its existance. It reminds us of Monty Python's Black Knight who loses all his arms and legs. "It's just a flesh wound."

Quarantini

One day we'll order this fancy named cocktail at a bar and look back and toast the bastard year that was 2020. Right now, a quarantini is whatever the hell you have in your liquor cabinet mixed up and downed like it's your last drink on earth. It could well be.

Zoombombing

Unwanted intrusions on your Zoom call. It's funny how in those incredibly boring real-life meetings in the old world, we never had strangers off the street suddenly burst in and say 'surprise'.

Bubble

Bubble was such an innocent word. Children blowing bubbles. Bubble bath. Bubble tea. Let's take back the bubble word and burst the 2020 bubble.

Quaranteam

It's not a nice word. Picking your team to quarantine with is like a bad high school sports game where you have to pick players to share a tent with for 3 months. Especially when you're the last to be picked because of your acne and smelly feet.

Maskne

Thought things couldn't get worse? Well they did. Wearing that mask and being a good global citizen gave you Maskne, or acne. What's next, life? Bring it on...

Fatten the Curve

This can be used to describe the copious amounts of food and drink consumed in lockdown as well as COVIDIOTS who decided it would be fun to go out and spread the virus. Yes, some people really suck.

Quarantine Hustle

Used to describe what we did to survive in quarantine. Some worked many virtual jobs, some started brand new vocations and completely retrained themselves. Many showed the best side of the human spirit and did what they had to survive. We salute you.

The 'Rona

We had so much time on our hands in 2020 of course we came up with an abbreviation for Coronavrius. Time well spent social media.

Virtual Happy Hour

Many of us haven't seen work colleagues for months. Virtual Happy Hours became the new normal. Toasting to colleagues on your laptop, spilling wine on your keyboard and passing out with your camera still on. Good times.

Corona Bae

Also known as "quarantine bae." Someone you dated in lockdown because you had watched everything on Netflix and had nothing else to do. You would never date this kind of person in a 'normal' world either. So you end up Zumping?

Zumping

It's as bad as it sounds. Getting dumped by Zoom. There's nothing good about it. Especially if you have a bad internet connection and you are the one being dumped. Let's hope this word disappears in 2020. Bring back ghosting.

Doomscrolling

Most of us did it. Endless scrolling on Facebook, Twitter and other social media feeds. Sometimes ending up in very weird places, watching a cross dressing pig skateboard at 2am or reading endless conspiracy theories about Bill Gates putting a chip in our brain so we can play solitaire with our eyes closed.

COVID-10

Yes, it's those 10 lbs you gained watching Tiger King and thinking 'finally something crazier than the news to distract me from real life.'

Tiger King

Definitely worth gaining 10 lbs and binge watching. Maybe the only good thing that came out of 2020.

Covidivorce

For some, quarantine with a loved one proved too much and Covidivorce became a thing. Seeing your partner 24/7 can take a toll on the tightest of relationships, especially if they are sitting in their sweatpants, gaining weight and binge watching The Great British Bake Off for six months.

Coronababy

Whilst some divorced, some procreated. The result, a lot of new babies coming into this world. Let's just hope it's a nicer world.

Work From Home (WFH)

Before 2020, WFH was something you saw on TV when people sat on a beach with a laptop and said they were a 'blogger' and you wondered how the hell they paid their rent. Now WFH is the new norm. We have ring lights to make us look good on video calls and green screen backgrounds so everyone can pretend to do the weather forecast.

Quaranteen

Maybe not the best label, but some drew the short straw of being a teenager during COVID. You couldn't run away, the government gave you a curfew and you couldn't date. Welcome to being a teenager.

Covid Party

As sick as it sounds (and it is), some thought it would be a good idea to have a party and try to catch COVID. These people consider the Dumb and Dumber movie too intellectual.

Pandemic

No one had ever uttered this word before unless you had two PhDs and spent your life looking down a microscope at alien looking creatures swimming around in a petri dish. Jeff Goldblum is also lined up to play you in a movie.

Coronacation

We went on vacation in our back gardens, in our living rooms, our bathrooms. We packed suitcases, put on sunscreen and walked all of ten feet to get to our Coronacation destination. The only plus side? No airport security and if you didn't like the service where you stayed, you only have yourself to blame. Maybe give your bathroom 2 stars on TripAdvisor.

New Normal

We didn't like this new phrase and we certainly didn't like the outcome. Let's go back to when normal was safe and boring, not something new and scary that could kill you.

Coronapocalypse

Once you've finished Doomscrolling this can often be your mental state. The feeling that the end of the world is nigh. That the virus is going to wipe out everyone. Or even worse, no more toilet roll for the rest of your life and you have to buy a bidet and speak French.

Learning Pod

Unless you have rich friends you may not have heard of this term. Some families who had to homeschool thought a private teacher living in their bubble was the best thing to avoid having to interact with and educate their own children. And so we have Learning Pods. You're welcome 2020.

Balcony Concerts

We saw some incredible acts of humanity with communities coming together in unprecedented ways. Concerts on roofs and balconies. Strangers playing together over Zoom. This may be one thing we actually miss when the new normal goes back to the old normal. Rather than give you inspiring concerts, your neighbours will leave you rude notes about the volume of your TV.

Contact Tracing

This term was reserved for those awkward conversations with ex's when you found out you had a STD. We can't wait for the day when you go to a restaurant and don't have to worry about who just sat in your seat or if that cough on the neighbouring table could actually kill your granny.

Community Spread

This sounds like it should be on the Monopoly board. But you don't get $200 if you pass this one on.

"Can everyone mute themselves"

Some awful things happened on video calls this year. Too many people had no idea how the cameras worked, how to mute themselves and all hell broke loose. Some even lost their job because of their IT ineptitude.

Taskforce

The A team were a taskforce. Thunderbirds were a taskforce. Suddenly politicians and scientists formed taskforces around the world and everyday people became potential saviors of the world. Only some failed miserably and some taskforces became a joke force. A very unfunny one.

Droplet

How did one innocent, simple word become so deadly that the entire world is scared of breathing in a single droplet. Sorry droplet, but we now collectively hate you and never want to hear your name again. No hard feelings.

Social Shaming

Let's be honest, this has happened for eternity only in different forms. Your grumpy old neighbour staring at you when you step on their grass, people leaving notes on your windscreen when you park badly. But now, it's ok. Covid has given the world the power of shaming. If you see someone who doesn't distance or wear a mask, you suddenly feel like a superhero with super shaming powers and you're going to use them. Make the most of it while you can.

Hydroxychloroquine

It's hard to say. It doesn't work. It never did. Let's just never say this ridiculous word ever again.

"Inject with bleach"

2020 came up with some really dumb ideas. This has to be in the top 5. Enough said.

Endemic

Pandemic and endemic can go take a hike. They can get married, have babies and move to Mars for all we care. No more things that end in 'emic' please.

Herd Immunity

Herds are for cows and elephants. Let's give this word back to them. Herds and people don't go well together. And herd immunity didn't work. It was a terrible idea. It could only be worse if we did herd immunity and gave everyone bleach to swig on.

Super-Spreader

No one wants to be a super-spreader unless you are in the final of the world peanut butter spreading competition. Then being a super-spreader is cool and will definitely impress your friends and family for at least a day.

Drive-Through Testing

Drive-throughs used to be fun. You arrive hungry, leave bloated. And minimal human interaction. Now drive-throughs involve getting a swab stuck up your nose to tickle your brain. And you don't get two warm cookies for a dollar to go with it.

Wash Your Hands

Nowhere in the history of hand washing has hand washing become so front and centre of everything we do. Our collective hands have never been so clean, so scrubbed, so full of sanitizer. We can't wait to have dirty hands again.

Outbreak

This title was a harmless 1995 American medical disaster film starring Dustin Hoffman, described as "a frustratingly uneven all-star disaster drama" by Rotten Tomatoes. See also, some members of the Taskforce.

Personal Protective Equipment (PPE)

No one knew about it. Then no one could buy it. That sums up PPE in 2020.

N95

This word should be a highway. Something with stunning views of lakes and mountains with a truck stop that serves gourmet food and vintage wine. Instead, it stands for a mask none of us has seen or can buy. It's a ghost for 2020.

Stimulus Check

Not only did we have to stay home, homeschool and search the internet for toilet paper, we got sent a check by the government to spend on toilet paper that we couldn't find. You can't make this sh*t up.

'Speaking moistly'

You could be forgiven for not knowing what this means. Many still don't. Canadian Prime Minister Justin Trudeau used the term to describe how important face masks were. He said wearing masks can prevent people from "breathing or speaking moistly." We never need to hear that phrase again.

Local Lockdown

As if the term lockdown wasn't bad enough, it had to go and spawn a local version of itself. So your friends could go out and take annoying Instagram pictures while you're stuck in your local hell of a lockdown with your snoring Parrot.

Unprecedented

Things that are unprecedented are rarely good. We've heard this term too many times in 2020. We like precedent. It makes us feel safe and secure. When you push the brakes, you want to know that they are going to work. There's a precedent. Unprecedented brakes aren't good. We look forward to a life of precedent once again.

Trying Times

How about we don't have any more trying times? Life is hard enough as it is. We don't need to add to the already long list of trying times life deals us. So we propose 2021 is trying time free. We all deserve a mental health year.

Bat Soup

We know this didn't cause the virus but it didn't stop this term becoming popular in 2020 and conspiracy theories running wild. Bat soup should be something only Batman eats. That's it. End of story.

Asymptomatic

Also known as the lucky ones. Wouldn't it be nice if every illness was asymptomatic? We wouldn't mind the word sticking around if we can achieve that.

Blursday

Lockdown can play wonders with your mind. Many experienced Blursday - when you literally have no idea what day of the week it is. You've lived in your pyjamas for weeks and haven't even looked in the mirror to see the slice of pizza stuck in your hair for the last three days.

False Positive

No one likes this term. It doesn't make sense. It shouldn't exist. It just gives those who believe in Fake News the encouragement that right can in fact can be wrong. Let's live a false positive free life.

Contactless

Contactless went from a niche credit card trend to a way of life for everyone. Contactless relationships, contactless sex, contactless shopping. For germaphobes it's the miracle they've been praying for all these years. For everyone else, it sucked.

QAnon

This digital cult became a household name with theories like the virus was a Chinese bioweapon or that its spread was designed by Democrats to prevent Trump's re-election. If only we could go back to the old conspiracies of who shot JR? They seemed so much tamer back then.

Covexit

Covexit is all about how we get out of the 'new normal' and back to the old normal. And then we will have to think of something new to complain about. Like how we miss the lockdowns or the fact we have to buy all new work clothes because of the COVID-10 weight we gained.

"When can I hug again?"

This is one of the saddest phrases of 2020. We've all missed hugging loved ones, friends and even people we don't like very much. That lack of close contact has been hard on the whole world. Unless you have intimacy issues, in which case it has been the year of your dreams.

Patient Zero

No one wants to be patient zero, especially when in this case it kills millions of people. Being patient zero is like being the person who pushes the nuclear button. No one is going to thank you, no one is going to give you the key to the city and Tom Cruise will never play you in a movie.

Zoom Fatigue

Too much Zooming is bad for the soul. When you are Zooming for work, going to an art gallery on Zoom and then attending a Zoom funeral all in the same day, life can feel a little distant. Zoom fatigue is real and is making therapists a lot of money. Well done 2020.

Stay Indoors

We don't mind hearing these words if it's a cold, rainy Sunday and you just want to stay in bed and watch an entire season of Schitt's Creek. But it's no fun when 2020 is essentially a stay indoors year. That's not a nice year.

Micro-Cluster

Yet another new term. Whether a micro cluster is better than a local lockdown, we may never know but they are both not good news. Micro-Cluster certainly won't be a popular baby name in 2021 unless you really hate your child.

Ventilator

No one foresaw companies like GM and Ford producing ventilators as part of their 2020 lineup. For a brief period, the spirit of the war years was embraced and companies changed their production lines for the common good. Then, everyone wanted to buy a new pick-up with their stimulus checks so they went back to making two ton gas-guzzlers.

"Out of an abundance of caution"

This phrase preceded pretty much every bad announcement in 2020. Out of an abundance of caution, we are shutting down the country. Out of an abundance of caution, I'm divorcing you. Out of an abundance of caution, you're fired. Out of an abundance of caution, I have to tell you, you're adopted.

China Virus

Calling anything after a country, especially with such negative connotations, is simply xenophobic and creates racial tensions. Don't do it. It's not nice.

PCR Test

We want to forget this word. Forget having our brains fondled by a swab. The term PCR should be re-imagined as 'Pink Coloring Rhino Test', to see if Rhino's like the color pink. What we'll do with that information, I don't care and it doesn't matter. It just sounds a lot nicer.

Hunker Down

Hunker Down used to be a stupid game played at hurricane parties. You watch the weather report and each time the meteorologist says "hunker down" you took a shot. If we took a shot every time we've been told to "hunker down" in 2020, we would pass out until 2021. On second thoughts, that may not be a bad idea...

"Nice to meet you, virtually"

At first, back in the 90s, this was a fun thing to say on your first ever video conference call. It got a little tiring in the 2000s but we still smiled when someone said it. In 2020 we're so over it. There's just no need. We all know it's virtual. The joke is over 21 years old. It can drink on its own now.

Curfew

The new C word. We aren't used to being told when to go to bed. Yes, it was for our own good and yes, it helped save lives, but no one liked it. We should never hear this word again until we are 100 years old in a nursing home, watching reruns of Casablanca and drooling constantly.

"Once this is over"

A term we tell ourselves on a daily basis. Once this is over, we will travel the world, we will live life with a renewed gusto, we will be grateful every day, we will be nice to our neighbours, we will never take anything for granted, ever again. Or we may just keep the beard, work from home permanently and become a hermit for the rest of our lives. Either works.

Miley Cyrus

As if coming up with The 'Rona wasn't enough, we had time to come up with cockney rhyming slang for the virus too. Miley Cyrus = Coronavirus. Yet another milestone for 2020.

Zoonotic

Not a Zoo that's in a trance. This new term references a disease that was originally detected in animals, but is now infecting people. So if you come home from a crazy Zoonotic night, best to call the CDC, and your Doctor, and isolate for the rest of your life.

Incubation Period

For the alien in your stomach it's a mere 24 hours. But for COVID, it's 2-14 days. Let's say goodbye to incubation periods. Period.

WHO

The WHO was something we all knew about but didn't really take an interest in, if we're really honest. 2020 made the WHO one of the most important bodies on the planet, for the survival of the planet. Now we'll take a bit more notice. And Roger Daltrey will no doubt sell a few more albums to those who Google incorrectly.

Essential Workers

They're amazing. So many owe their lives to them. They are braver than most of us will ever be. If you're an essential worker, we love you and we thank you. Sorry we didn't quite realize how much you do before 2020. We suck.

Remdesivir

Never worked for COVID according to the WHO despite being touted by many for PR distractions from the growing national crisis. Also a silly name. Remdesivir and Hydroxychloroquine should just go into exile. They can play chess together and swap funny anecdotes about how people thought they would save the planet.

"Now more than ever"

Closely related to 'out of an abundance of caution', this phrase has been way overused in 2020. Now, more than ever, we need this phrase to die.

Boomer Remover

A disgusting term used mainly by Covidiots to describe the virus because the Boomer Baby age group between the ages of 56 and 74 were the most susceptible. We never need to hear that term again.

Animal-Human Interface

How we interact with animals and potentially spread disease. This does not mean going out to dinner with a Monkey and sharing Bat soup over a romantic candlelit dinner. We certainly don't recommend that. Maybe just meet for drinks first. And never ghost a Monkey. They get very upset.

Rigged Election

Wasn't it nice that we got to [insert age] and in all these years, never had to listen to rigged election news for weeks on end. Let's hope and pray it's the last time we hear it. It's the icing on a 2020 disaster cake.

"Apply light and heat"

When the President suddenly comes up with an ad hoc potential cure for the virus by "applying light and heat" you know 2020 has gone off the rails. Unfortunately, despite the best medical minds spending at least two seconds looking into it, applying light and heat did not work.

Long Covid

Just when you think there is nothing else 2020 can come up to really screw with us, it does. Not only do we have Covid, we have long term effects of Covid. I mean, really? We still don't know the full effects of long term Covid, but we're pretty sure you don't get any super powers from it.

Blood Oxygen Levels

In 2020 we all became doctors. We took our temperature more times than we can count. We bought Oxymeters and surgical gloves. We performed minor heart surgeries on our loved ones on the kitchen table as we were too scared to take them to the hospital.

Convalescent Plasma Therapy

A great name for a thrash metal band. We're still not sure if it actually works or not. CPT shows 2020 can surprise us every day with a new acronym we're more than eager to forget in 2021.

Emergency Use Authorization

This sounds like an order Darth Vader would issue to fire the Death Star laser even though it's not quite tested and there are still a few nuts and bolts left on the floor. Now we're hoping emergency use authorization will save the planet from the virus. Fingers crossed. If you're a visiting alien reading this and there's no one else alive, we may have screwed up.

Viral Shedding

We've all become potential shedders against our will. No one wants to be a shedder. It sounds bad, it is bad. Let's have a shed free life in 2021 and beyond. In fact, let's get rid of the word entirely or turn it into some kind of weird mating act where you cover your naked loved one in cheese? Yes, that's definitely better.

Dalgona Coffee

A beautiful Korean coffee that gained Instagram notoriety because of 2020. We don't know why, but it looks nice. Google it.

An Obese Turtle

Anderson Cooper famously described President Trump as "an obese turtle on his back, flailing in the hot sun, realizing his time is over." Hopefully the same can be said for 2020. It's been an awful year and it's time for 2020 to die.

COVID-19 / CORONAVIRUS

Excuse our French, but fuck you Covid. No one likes you. No one will ever like you. If we could tie Coronavirus up in the Pulp Fiction basement and set Marsellus on it, we would. And Bruce Willis could say "'Rona's dead baby. 'Rona's dead." End scene.

The End.

And we hope, back to a new old normal. Stay safe everyone.

Epilogue

As we stated at the beginning of this book, we hope no one took offense and for a few minutes we helped bring some laughter and cheer to what has been such a crappy year. We're all exhausted, mentally, physically, emotionally. Some of us have had the worst years of our lives. At the time of writing over 1.4 million people have died with over 60 million confirmed cases worldwide.

Some governments around the world have failed on a monumental scale. Some performed incredibly well in protecting their citizens. History will look back and analyze what went wrong and hopefully future generations will learn from this global tragedy. The important thing is to keep hope alive.

No matter how bad things get, things will get better. There is hope on the horizon. Vaccines are on the way and by the end of 2021 we hope COVID-19 is no longer a part of our daily lives. We can slowly return to work, we can go out without a mask, stand close to people, breathe in the fresh air and most importantly, we can hug again.

So whatever cards 2020 has dealt you, life will get better. There is always hope and there is a hug waiting for you at the end of this rainbow.

Terms and Phrases used in this Book

Quarantine
The 'R' Number
Flattening the Curve
Social Distancing 6ft Rule
Lockdown
Zoom
Masks
Vaccine
Antibodies
Maskhole
Shitshow
Quarantine and Chill
CDC
Covidiot
Moronavirus
Quarantini
Zoombombing
Bubble
Quaranteam
Maskne
Fatten the Curve
Quarantine Hustle
The 'Rona
Virtual Happy Hour
Corona Bae
Zumping
Doomscrolling
COVID-10
Tiger King
Covidivorce
Coronababy
Work From Home (WFH)
Quaranteen
Covid Party
Pandemic
Coronacation

New Normal
Coronapocalypse
Learning Pod
Balcony Concerts
Contact Tracing
Community Spread
"Can everyone mute themselves"
Taskforce
Droplet
Social Shaming
Hydroxychloroquine
"Inject with bleach"
Endemic
Herd Immunity Super-Spreader
Drive-Through Testing
Wash Your Hands
Outbreak
Personal Protective Equipment (PPE)
N95
Stimulus Check
'Speaking moistly'
Local Lockdown
Unprecedented
Trying Times
Bat Soup
Asymptomatic
Blursday
False Positive
Contactless
QAnon
Covexit
"When can I hug again?"
Patient Zero
Zoom Fatigue
Stay Indoors
Micro-Cluster
Ventilator
"Out of an abundance of caution"

China Virus
PCR Test
Hunker Down
"Nice to meet you, virtually"
Curfew
"Once this is over"
Miley Cyrus
Zoonotic
Incubation Period
WHO
Essential Workers
Remdesivir
"Now more than ever"
Boomer Remover
Rigged Election
Animal-Human Interface
"Apply light and heat"
Long Covid
Blood Oxygen Levels
Convalescent Plasma Therapy
Emergency Use Authorization Dalgona Coffee
Viral Shedding
An Obese Turtle
COVID-19 / CORONAVIRUS

And yes, we didn't list every word. There's a new one every day - like quarantine fatigue. But at some point we had to stop, take a breath and get back to the new normal.

Still bored? Now you've learned a few new phrases, why not try our word search. It will help kill a few more minutes before the vaccine.

Covid Word Search

```
M  M  Z  R  C  V  T  Q  U  A  R  A  N  T  I  N  I  C
A  M  O  U  O  C  P  C  D  C  C  Z  L  H  B  J  A  O
S  A  R  R  M  C  O  V  I  D  I  V  O  R  C  E  N  V
K  S  O  G  O  P  L  R  M  A  S  K  H  O  L  E  T  I
N  K  N  C  F  N  I  D  O  W  B  Z  O  O  M  C  I  D
E  S  A  E  S  F  A  N  W  N  N  N  D  J  V  Q  B  I
C  S  E  Z  O  L  S  V  G  Q  A  O  Z  P  B  B  O  O
Z  O  O  M  B  O  M  B  I  N  G  B  A  K  W  W  D  T
Q  L  O  C  K  D  O  W  N  R  T  K  A  E  J  F  I  Y
Q  U  A  R  A  N  T  E  A  M  U  M  R  B  E  H  E  M
C  W  V  A  C  C  I  N  E  P  E  S  Z  K  Y  H  S  O
H  B  U  B  B  L  E  Q  U  A  R  A  N  T  I  N  E  I
```

Find the following words in the puzzle.
Words are hidden → ↓ and ↘ .

ANTIBODIES	MASKHOLE	RONA
BUBBLE	MASKNE	VACCINE
CDC	MASKS	WFH
CORONABABY	MORONAVIRUS	ZOOM
COVIDIOT	QUARANTEAM	ZOOMBOMBING
COVIDIVORCE	QUARANTINE	ZUMPING
LOCKDOWN	QUARANTINI